More books about Kipper:

Kipper
Kipper's Toybox
Kipper's Birthday
Kipper's Snowy Day
Kipper's Christmas Eve
Kipper's A to Z
Kipper's Monster
Kipper and Roly
Kipper's Beach Ball
One Year with Kipper
Hide Me, Kipper
Kipper Story Collection
Kipper's Birthday
and Other Stories

HODDER CHILDREN'S BOOKS

First published in Great Britain in 2014 by Hodder & Stoughton
This paperback edition first published in 2015

5 7 9 10 8 6 4

Text and illustrations copyright © Mick Inkpen, 2014

The moral rights of the author and illustrator have been asserted.

A CIP catalogue record for this book
is available from the British Library.

ISBN: 978 1 444 93699 5

Printed in China

Hodder Children's Books
An imprint of
Hachette Children's Group
Part of Hodder & Stoughton Limited
Carmelite House
50 Victoria Embankment
London,EC4Y 0DZ

An Hachette UK Company
www.hachette.co.uk

www.hachettechildrens.co.uk

Kipper's Little Friends

Mick Inkpen

Hodder
Children's
Books

A division of Hachette Children's Books

Arnold was proudly showing
Kipper his new toy baby owl.
It was very small.
And grey. And fluffy.
'We could call your owl. . .
Small Grey Fluffy Owl,'
said Kipper.
It was not a very
inventive name.
A bit long too.
But Arnold
seemed pleased.

'Big Owl . . . and Small Grey Fluffy Owl,' said Kipper.

'I wonder what a baby owl is called?' said Kipper.
'You are a baby pig.
And a baby pig is called a piglet.
So perhaps a baby owl is called...
an Owlet!'

Kipper looked at his computer.

'Yes!' said Kipper.
'A baby owl is an owlet.'

'And look! A baby frog is...
a froglet!'

He read some more.

'And a baby hedgehog is...
a hoglet!'

K ipper was very pleased
with himself.

'Piglet. Owlet. Froglet.
Hoglet,' he said.
'Let's go to the park and
see if we can find some
hoglets and froglets!'

They couldn't find any hoglets in the park. And there were no froglets in the pond.

Just some wriggly things in the stinky mud.

But the ducks were there as usual. And five baby ducks were paddling in the pond too.

Arnold wondered if
Small Grey Fluffy Owl
would like to paddle with them . . .

...splish!

Small Grey Fluffy Owl
spun slowly on his back,
and began to sink.

The baby ducks, thinking he
was a piece of bread, paddled over
to dabble at him.

'Shoooo!' said
Kipper, and dipped
his net into
the water.

S mall Grey Fluffy Owl
wasn't very fluffy any more.
And he seemed even smaller
than before.

A bit stinky too.

But Arnold didn't seem
to notice. He had discovered
something interesting in the net.

A tiny froglet!

It crawled onto
Arnold's finger. . .

stared at him for a while. . .

then hopped onto his nose . . .

and jumped back into the pond . . .

. . . ploop!

They sat on the swings,
swooshing backwards
and forwards, while Kipper
spun Small Grey Fluffy Owl
around to dry him out.

'What is the name for
a baby duck?' said Kipper.
'Piglet. Owlet. Froglet. Hoglet.
It must be. . .

ducklet!'

It didn't sound right.

B ack home Kipper looked at his computer again.
'Silly me! A baby duck is called a **duckling!**
Of course it is!' said Kipper.

'And look, Arnold!
A baby goose is called a **gosling.**
I didn't know that.

And goslings are grey and fluffy too!'

They drew pictures of all the baby animals and wrote the names underneath.

owlet

froglet

piglet

hoglet

duckling   gosling

Then Kipper drew a picture of himself and wrote **dog**.

dog

'**W**hat was I when I was little?' said Kipper.
'Was I a. . .

doglet. . .

or a **dogling?**'

Silly Kipper. He had forgotten
the name for a baby dog.
Do you know the name
for a baby dog?
Of course you do.
A baby dog is a. . .

. . . .puppy.

And this is what
Kipper looked like
when Big Owl was
brand new,
and Kipper was
just a puppy.